THE LONG-LOST SECRET DIARY OF THE WORLD'S WORST SAMURAI

SCRIBO

a SALARIYA imprint

First published in Great Britain by Scribo MMXX
Scribo, an imprint of
The Salariya Book Company
25 Marlborough Place, Brighton, BN1 1UB

ISBN 978-1-913337-17-9

The right of Tim Collins to be identified as the author of this work has
been asserted in accordance with sections 77 and 78 of the Copyright,
Designs and Patents Act, 1988.

Book Design by David Salariya

Printed and bound in China

The text for this book is set in Century Schoolbook
The display type is Jacob Riley

www.salariya.com

Artwork Credits
Illustrations: Isobel Lundie

THE LONG-LOST SECRET DIARY OF THE WORLD'S WORST SAMURAI

Written by
Tim Collins

Illustrated by
Isobel Lundie

SCRIBO
a SALARIYA *imprint*

Chapter I

—

Japan, 1582

I'm going to be a samurai!

Day One

Mother thinks I'm practising my writing. I do it every day and she never reads it. So while I kneel here in my silk robe, dabbing my brush onto the paper like an obedient daughter, I'm going to reveal my true destiny.

I, Suki Akiyama, am going to become a samurai warrior. My father is one, and my brother is training to become one. It's in my blood.

Mother thinks I'm going to help her with the fish soon, but I'm not. I'm going to take my bamboo stick up to the jagged rocks, and train myself to become a fearsome fighter.

My family won't need me to chop up fish if our daimyo calls us to battle. They'll need me to chop up enemies.

GET REAL

Women in medieval Japan were brought up to serve their fathers, and eventually their husbands. But some chose a life of violent battle instead. Female warriors who fought alongside men were known as 'Onna-Bugeisha'.

Day Two

Mother couldn't find me when she needed me to slice the fish yesterday, so now I'm forbidden to go outside. She's standing behind me in her green silk robe, with her neat hair tied back, her black eyes fixed on me and her small mouth fixed in a scowl.

I don't think she's reading what I'm writing, though. Let me test it.

I'm still going to be a samurai. She can't stop me. No one can.

My true place is charging into battle and beheading enemies, not preparing food and sweeping floors.

When I was out on the jagged rocks yesterday, I told myself I was a samurai and it felt right.

The rocks are to the north of our village, and
they overlook the main path, which winds down
a steep hill, and eventually takes you all the
way to the coast.

I held up my bamboo stick and pretended to be
a fearsome warrior, facing hordes of enemies
armed with swords, lances, bows and arrows.

In my imagination, the stick became a long, curved sword that was created by a master craftsman. As the waves of enemies came at me, I sliced their heads off and added them to my collection. I soon gathered over a hundred, each with an identical expression of terror mixed with grudging respect.

The final line of enemies surged forward in a last, desperate attempt to beat me, but I rushed out to meet them with my blade so high that the sky itself was carved in two.

I heard a ripping noise, which took me out of my fantasy. I turned around and saw I'd torn the back of my robe on one of the jagged rocks.

I knew that honesty is part of the way of the samurai, so I trekked home and admitted what I'd done to Mother.

If anything, she was even more ferocious than the enemies I'd been imagining. She told me to mend my robe, and stay inside from now on.

But she can't stop me practising my samurai skills. I know I'll need them one day.

Day Three

My father and my brother Yasutaro have arrived home, and I can hear them talking in the next room. At 13, Yasutaro is a year younger than me, yet he was the one chosen to go to samurai school. It's bad enough to imagine him there, learning all those amazing skills, but it's even worse when he returns home and boasts about it.

He says he's doing brilliantly, but I bet I'd do even better if I were given the chance. He's just finished intense training with a teacher called

Yoshihiro, a samurai who Father has fought alongside many times. This teacher has been very strict, and pushed him very hard, but he's come out of it as a great fighter, or so he says.

Mother and Father were distracted by Yasutaro, so at least I could sneak away and practise my sword skills again. I bet I could beat my brother in a battle, despite all of his fancy training.

Day Four

Yasutaro is telling Father all about the military tactics he's learned. Father is stroking his moustache and questioning him about imaginary battle situations. Yasutaro is scratching his head and dispensing wisdom like he's a veteran of a hundred battles, even though he hasn't been in a single one.

Father has the traditional samurai hairstyle which is shaved at the front with a small topknot. Yasutaro isn't old enough for this yet. His black hair is still short and spiky. But soon, if his teachers let him, he'll go through the coming-of-age ceremony and he'll be allowed samurai hair too.

I can't bear to hear Yasutaro discussing tactics. I'd be so much better than him if someone just gave me the chance.

I always beat him whenever we were playing Go. I could always second guess what he was going to do. If I was in charge of an army, I'd outthink any opponent.

GET REAL

Go is thought to be the oldest board game that is still regularly played. It was invented over 2,500 years ago in China, and was very popular in medieval Japan.

One player uses white stones, while the other uses black ones. They take turns placing them on a board to try and surround the largest area. They can also capture their opponent's stones by surrounding them. The player who has taken the most territory and removed the most enemy stones wins.

Day Five

I finally did it. As Father, Mother, Yasutaro and I were eating our morning rice, I stood up and announced I was going to be a samurai.

Yasutaro laughed, and I had to stop myself from throwing my bowl at him. I don't know much about the code of the samurai, but I'm guessing that attacking your own brother during a meal probably isn't part of it.

Mother told me to stop talking nonsense and get on with my chores.

I was expecting Father to say something similar, but he didn't. He froze with his rice bowl in his hand and peered at me in silence. Then he asked why I wanted to be a samurai.

I told him I was from a great samurai family, and it wasn't fair that Yasutaro got to be one and I didn't.

Father nodded and asked if I had any other reason.

I said I was better at fighting than Yasutaro, and if I could be sent to Yoshihiro I would emerge as the true warrior of our family.

Father nodded and asked if I had any other reason.

I said I was better at tactics than Yasutaro, and one day I could become a great commander and lead troops to glorious victories.

Father finished his rice in silence. When his bowl was empty, he said he refused to send me to samurai school.

I tried to keep my anger in, but it was no use. I said it was ridiculous that he wouldn't let me train just because I was a girl.

Father laughed. He said that wasn't the reason, and there were many stories about female samurai who'd commanded armies of thousands. He said the reason he wouldn't send me was because I wasn't thinking like a true samurai should.

Mother repeated her demand for me to get back to my duties, but Father said I could be excused for one day. He told me to take the time to think and then answer the question again tomorrow morning.

GET REAL

Female samurai were rare, but some became legendary figures whose stories were repeated long after they died. An epic account of 12th century battles called The Tale of the Heike *describes a female warrior called Tomoe Gozen. It says she was 'fit to confront a demon or a god' and 'worth a thousand warriors'.*

Day Six

I spent yesterday wandering around our village and thinking about my answer. Only a few people live here. There are five other samurai, plus their wives, plus a few elderly people and some children who are much younger than me.

One of the old men, Fujioka, asked me what the problem was. I told him I was trying to work out how to answer an important question, and he said I should just tell the truth, as it was always better in the long run. I bowed and thanked him for his advice.

Another of the old men, called Kuroki, said that lying could lead to many problems, but so could telling the truth, because life was full of pain and if I didn't believe him I should try coping with his back. I didn't bother to thank him.

I paced around the whole village, from the rice fields on either side and the edges of the dense forests beyond, to the steep cliffs that rose up on the south.

I tried to work out what Father wanted to hear.

At first I couldn't get my angry, jealous thoughts about Yasutaro out of my mind. But I already knew Father didn't see these as a good enough reason to become a samurai.

Maybe I could explain how good I thought I could be without being mean about Yasutaro? But it would still sound boastful.

What did he want me to say? That I was brave enough to be a samurai? Or obedient enough to train with that strict teacher?

Then I remembered something Father says before leaving for battle. He doesn't talk about how great he is at fighting, or how certain he is of winning, he just says it's his duty.

That seemed like the sort of thing I should say.

After we finished our rice and bean curd this morning, Father gave me the chance to answer again. He asked why I wanted to become a samurai, and I said it didn't matter if I wanted to or not. I had to do it because it was my duty.

He nodded and said I'd answered well. He said this was a much more honourable reason than envy or personal glory.

He asked if I could swear to be respectful, honest and brave, and I said I could. Then he said that I could return to the school with them, and he'd ask Yoshihiro to take me on for fifty days. At the end of that time, the teacher would decide if I was worth keeping on.

My brother grumbled that Yoshihiro wouldn't want to train me just because I'm good at Go and told Father what he wanted to hear, but Father told him to be quiet. He said he had battled alongside Yoshihiro many times, and he would agree to his request.

I thanked Father and bowed.

I worked out the correct answer to Father's question, but I wasn't being totally honest, even though a samurai is meant to be. The truth is, I do want a little bit of personal glory. Well, a lot really. Okay, I'll admit it. I want to be the mightiest and most glorious warrior in the whole world.

GET REAL

The code of the samurai was known as Bushido. It demanded obedience, honesty, respect, courage, self-control and dedication to duty. The principles of Bushido are still hugely popular in Japan, in much the same way that the notion of chivalry lives on in Europe. Modern Japanese people might follow Bushido in the workplace rather than the battlefield, but it's basically the same thing, only with more spreadsheets and less gushing blood.

Day Seven

We set off early this morning. I tied my sleeping mat to my back and followed Father and Yasutaro along the path that leads through a narrow gap in the jagged rocks and down the hill.

We soon turned into another path that forked off to the right, and Father said we could follow this one all the way to the school.

While Father strode on ahead, Yasutaro hung back and told me horror stories about Yoshihiro's teaching methods. He says he makes you train all day, and if you collapse with exhaustion, you have to clean the entire hall with a brush that only has three bristles.

He says Yoshihiro won't go right ahead and teach you how to use a sword or fire arrows. He'll make you do weird tasks first, and if you fail them, he'll say you aren't worth training.

Yasutaro and the others have already been through this hell, and they'll be based in the main hall with another teacher called Moriyori while Yoshihiro instructs me in the Zen garden, the side room and on the veranda.

I know my brother is just trying to put me off, but I have to admit I'm pretty worried.

But I'm sure it will be okay. I'll just have to call on the strength of my ancestors if I'm stuck. If they could survive years of real battles, I'm sure I can survive fifty days of training.

GET REAL

Zen gardens used rocks, water features, trees and bushes to create tranquil environments where samurai could relax and banish worries from their minds. The word 'Zen' comes from a branch of Buddhism which values self-control and intuition.

Day Eight

We've been walking on this path from dawn until dusk for two days now. My legs are aching and the straps of my sandals have rubbed so deep into my feet that they're surrounded by brown clumps of dried blood.

But I'm not going to complain. A true samurai never would. They could get both their legs chopped off in battle and they'd still keep on marching without grumbling.

I hope this journey lasts another ten days. I wouldn't care. I might just check with Father to find out how long it will be, though.

Day Nine

We can see the coast in the far distance, which means we'll arrive at the training school tomorrow. We've placed our mats down earlier than usual tonight because we've made such good progress.

Father has brought some rice cakes and honey for us to eat tonight, but I'm not sure I'll manage to stay awake long enough to get any.

It's more important that I get some proper rest before my training begins.

Chapter 2
⊢⎯⊣
Samurai school

Day Ten

The school is a long, flat building with white walls and a red roof, surrounded by a big wooden veranda.

There's a large exercise area at the front, and to the left there's a walled garden filled with cherry blossom trees, green shrubs and winding paths of smooth pebbles. There's a small round pond in the middle spanned by a low wooden bridge, and there's a row of miniature trees growing in pots to the left of it.

Most of the space inside the school is taken up by the training hall, but light walls of wood and paper mark out the sleeping quarters and the side room.

The other students were lined up in the main hall when we arrived. They were all boys, some younger than me with short, black hair and some of my age or older with shaved heads and topknots. They were holding wooden swords and standing with their feet apart.

They all turned to look at me.

A tall man with small eyes, grey hair and bushy eyebrows yelled at them to focus on their task and their eyes darted away again. I guessed the man must be Yoshihiro.

He was standing with a shorter man in a blue robe, who I took to be Moriyori. Father strode over to speak to them, and Yoshihiro fixed his gaze on me as they talked. I tried to stare back at his intense black eyes, but couldn't stop myself looking away.

After a few moments, Father returned and said Yoshihiro had agreed to train me for fifty days.

I thanked Father and bowed. I felt as though my whole life had been leading up to that moment, and I had a squirming feeling deep in my stomach as I thought about how badly I wanted to succeed. My hands were shaking, so I put them behind my back where the teacher couldn't see them.

Day Eleven

Moriyori showed me a small gap on the floor at the back of the sleeping quarters last night. It was just about big enough for me to unroll my mat and lie down.

I tried to relax. Bright moonlight was shining through the window right onto me. I felt like it was marking me out, bringing the awkward new girl to everyone's attention.

It turned out that I didn't need the Moon to pick me out. As Moriyori left, I heard two other pupils whispering about how long they thought I'd last with Yoshihiro. One of them said he'd give up on me after two days, but the other said he thought I could make it to three.

I sighed. If I let them get away with this sort of talk, it wasn't going to stop. Putting them in their place wouldn't make me popular, but I needed to do it.

I was about to tell them to shut up or I'd chop their heads off and use their hair to sweep the floor, but someone else spoke up first.

It was my brother. He said that Yoshihiro had agreed to train me, and if anyone had a problem with it they should tell him. He said they wouldn't find it easy to make jokes when he was making them lick the training yard clean with their tongues.

The giggling cut out and I thanked my brother in a low whisper.

It's strange that he spoke up for me after spending all that time frightening me on the way here. His rule must be that he's allowed to tease me, but no one else can.

Day Twelve

I woke up early this morning and watched the room fill with soft orange light as the Sun rose. I knew that today was going to be the start of my training, but I didn't know where I was meant to go or what I was meant to do.

I looked up at the neat wooden beams of the roof and wondered if I was meant to go and find Yoshihiro. Then a dark shape appeared in the corner of my eye, and when I looked around I saw he was standing right next to me.

He must have entered the room and stepped over all the other sleeping pupils without making a sound.

He strolled silently out again and I followed him.

I could hear my feet thudding across the floor and it made me wince to think how much heavier my tread was. I heard a loud, confused cry and realised I'd accidentally stomped on the hand of one of the sleeping students. I hoped Yoshihiro hadn't heard.

I found the teacher at the entrance to the

walled garden. He walked inside with his hands tucked neatly behind his back.

When he reached the pond, he turned and stared at me in silence. I wondered if I was meant to show initiative and start demonstrating my samurai skills. But after a while, he said Father had asked him to train me for a short period, and he'd agreed.

I took this as a cue to tell him all about how brilliant I would definitely be at sword-fighting and firing arrows.

Yoshihiro held his hand up and I stopped.

He said all that could come later, but first I had to learn how to be a warrior on the inside. He hit his own chest as he said this.

Then he picked up a small grey pebble and placed it in the palm of his hand. He told me to prove myself by grabbing it from him.

I squinted at him. I couldn't imagine how this skill would ever be useful in battle. Unless I were fighting an enemy who loved a pebble so much that they'd burst into tears if it was stolen from them.

I lunged forward and tried to grasp the stone. My hand swatted thin air. When I looked up, I saw that Yoshihiro was holding his hand high above his head.

It seemed impossible. I hadn't seen Yoshihiro move his hand at all. One moment it had been there and the next it was gone. It was as though it had disappeared and reappeared again somewhere else.

I would never have believed anyone could move that fast, never mind someone so thin and old.

Yoshihiro said we'd try it the other way around. He handed me the pebble and told me to stop him from grabbing it. I placed it in my palm and took a deep breath. This didn't sound too hard. All I'd have to do was clasp my hand as soon as I saw him move.

I told him to go ahead. His hand moved in a rapid blur, and my fingers slapped into an empty palm.

We tried again. I snapped my fingers shut sooner this time, but they still closed on thin air.

I asked Yoshihiro to give me one more chance. He agreed, and this time I smacked my hand shut even faster.

I gasped. There was something inside my hand. On just the first day of training I'd beaten his test. Here was proof that I was destined to be a great warrior.

I opened my hand. In the centre was a small pebble that had been painted red. For a moment, I wondered how it could have changed colour. Then Yoshihiro opened his own hand to reveal the original grey pebble. He hadn't just managed to take it this time, he'd switched it for a different one.

He bowed and walked away, leaving me to stare at the red pebble in shock.

Day Thirteen

Yoshihiro led me into the garden again today. He was carrying a large white jug with pink flowers painted on the side.

He plunged the jug into the pool and dripped the water back in very slowly. He said that a true samurai warrior would be able to pass their hand between the drops without getting it wet.

It was another task that didn't seem to relate to battle very much, but also didn't seem too tough.

I stepped up to the jug, held my hand flat and tried to swish it through. I could have sworn I'd aimed at a gap, but I felt the cold splash of water on my knuckles.

I tried again. And again. And again.

Finally, I had to admit I couldn't do it. My hand was getting soaked every time. I looked at Yoshihiro and saw that his blue robe was covered with dark splashes. There was even a drop of water running down his moustache.

He dropped the jug into the pond, bowed and then left.

Another failure, then. But so what? I want to fight enemies, not drops of water.

Day Fourteen

Yoshihiro guided me onto the veranda to the right of the school today. There was a long roll of thin rice paper unfurled there.

Yoshihiro removed his sandals and walked across without making a noise. Although the paper was incredibly thin and fragile, he left no mark.

Then he pointed to the paper and told me to try.

Again, it didn't seem too difficult. Yoshihiro was much taller than me, and although he was thin, he must have weighed a lot more. All I had to do was flit quickly across, and I was bound to leave the paper intact.

I took my sandals off and stepped across. I made no sound, and thought I'd been doing well until I looked over my shoulder and saw tiny rips where my feet had been.

I groaned, but there was still time to save it. If I left no mark on what was left, Yoshihiro might still count it as a win.

I tried to go on tiptoes, but could feel right away that I was tearing the paper.

I decided my best bet would be to bound across in huge leaps. I jumped high in the air, but landed awkwardly on my left foot, and crashed to the ground. The rice paper disintegrated as I landed on it.

Yoshihiro stepped over me and returned to the far end of the veranda. As he disappeared around the corner, he said I'd never be a samurai. He said he'd tested my reactions, my speed and my stealth, and I'd failed miserably on all counts.

My eyes were stinging. Father had convinced Yoshihiro to give me fifty days of training, but he'd only needed three. It was over already.

I couldn't even bring myself to get up. I just lay where I'd fallen and let my tears fall onto the torn rice paper.

Day Fifteen

Yoshihiro didn't come for me this morning.

I dressed and joined the others in the hall for rice and soya beans. I sat next to my brother and told him what had happened. He said Yoshihiro had never given up on anyone so soon, so I must be the worst pupil ever. I told him he'd made me feel a lot better, and jabbed him in the ribs with my chopstick.

He said the best thing I could do was sit in the Zen garden and reflect on what had gone wrong. Perhaps Yoshihiro would see how seriously I was taking it and decide to give me another try.

It was quite a good idea, for something that came from my brother.

When the bowls had been cleared away and the others began their training with Moriyori, I made my way to the garden.

I knelt in front of the pond and watched the gentle drift of the water lilies.

I tried to look like I was full of remorse, but the truth I was just angry. How was I meant to have grabbed the pebble from his hand when he's been practising for hundreds of years and it was my first try?

And I'm sure I would have got better at avoiding the drip of water and walking over the rice paper if I'd had time. He was meant to be training me, wasn't he? Doesn't that involve making allowances for some mistakes?

I felt my breathing getting faster and my cheeks getting hotter. I wanted to grab a sword and chop the bridge up so it could float in the pond right next to the stupid water lilies.

I heard a rustle near the door as if someone had walked past.

Was that Yoshihiro? Had he somehow sensed I was annoyed instead of remorseful?

Probably not. If it had been him, he'd have made no sound at all.

Day Sixteen

I didn't want to go back to the Zen garden today, so I decided to stay in the main hall after I'd finished my sliced trout in vinegar. I sat at the back with my head down, and nobody seemed to notice.

Today's lesson was very unusual. Moriyori announced that instead of teaching them combat skills, he'd be holding an endurance contest to see how much discomfort they could stand. He said that in a battle you have to fight on despite your injuries, and overcoming pain is a vital skill.

I wondered if he was going to stick needles into their hands or something, but the contest was actually very simple.

Moriyori lit a stick of incense with evenly-spaced notches down the side. He said that the winner would be the person who lasted the longest without blinking.

Yoshihiro wandered into the room and stood next to the incense. I cowered down so he wouldn't see me.

A tall boy went first. Moriyori sounded a gong and the boy stared at the class with his eyes wide. The sweet, rich smoke from the incense was drifting through the room, and it made me want to rub my eyes, so it must have been incredibly hard not to blink when you were right next to it.

The boy blinked and Moriyori announced he had lasted for two notches. A small boy with thick hair tried next, but blinked instinctively right away and grunted in frustration. An older boy in a green robe did much better. He stretched his cheeks and eyebrows apart, and lasted for four notches. By the time he finally closed his eyes they were bloodshot, and tears were streaming down his cheeks.

Other pupils tried, but none could beat his score.

I had an idea, and suddenly wished I could take part. I found myself staring at Moriyori when he was looking around for the next volunteer, and for a moment I forgot I wasn't meant to be there.

I heard Yoshihiro calling out my name, and I braced myself for him to get angry with me for sneaking in. But he actually asked if I'd like to try the challenge.

I stepped to the front, bowed at both teachers and thanked them for letting me take part. I could hear muttering and laughing from the crowd. Word had obviously spread about how badly I'd done so far.

I decided to approach the task differently from the others. I couldn't tell if I was cheating, or finding a clever way around the problem. Before Moriyori sounded the gong, I closed my eyes. And I kept them shut for the whole time. After all, how can you blink when your eyes aren't open in the first place?

I could hear the chatter of the other pupils as I stood in front of them with my eyes closed.

Moriyori shouted at me to complete the challenge properly, but Yoshihiro told me to stay as I was. Then he said I was teaching the others the valuable lesson that sometimes the answer is simpler than you think.

I stood there for a while longer, breathing the rich scent of jasmine smoke. Then Moriyori announced that I had lasted for five notches and I was the winner of the contest.

I opened my eyes again and bowed.

GET REAL

One of the ways time was measured in medieval Japan and China was by incense sticks. You could judge how much time had passed by how far the sticks had burned down. This simple principle led to elaborate 'incense clocks' with embedded bells that would fall after a certain amount of time. Some even used different types of incense so you could tell the time from the smell.

Chapter 3

A second chance

Day Seventeen

When I woke up this morning I saw Yoshihiro standing in the doorway and clutching a long bamboo stick. He beckoned me out onto the flat ground outside the school.

He said he was impressed with my performance in the contest. It showed I could think my way around problems, which is an important skill for battle.

Then he drew a rectangle on the floor and traced two larger shapes around it. He said it was a castle with a keep, an inner wall and an outer wall. He told me to imagine I was in charge of 400 samurai warriors inside, trying to protect it from 1,000 invaders, some of whom would be archers on horseback.

He marked out mountains behind the castle, and forests on either side. This layout made me think of our village, which made it easier to picture it.

I imagined myself in the tower, looking down at the enemy hordes as they swarmed towards me with their banners flying.

I said I wouldn't allow the enemy to draw me out into battle. That might seem brave, but it would ultimately lead to defeat.

Instead, I'd hold the castle, sending out small groups to dig pits in the ground for the enemies to fall into, lead them into the forest and trap them by chopping trees down, or lure them over to the mountains and pelt them with rocks.

Their archers and horses might look impressive, but eventually their arrows would run out and their horses would need hay and water.

Their numbers would dwindle, and soon it would be time to launch surprise night attacks on the remaining troops.

Yoshihiro nodded and scrubbed out his drawing. Then he sketched out some triangles which he explained were a high mountain range, and marked out a large plain in front of them. He asked how I would defend this territory from an army of mounted archers.

I said I'd retreat to the mountains and defend the passes. They would be too narrow for the horses to charge, and would provide cover from the arrows.

Yoshihiro nodded again and sketched an island base that I was meant to invade with a fleet of ships. I told him I'd attack from the front to lure the forces out, but send my best warriors to ambush from behind.

We went on like this all day, with Yoshihiro describing scenarios, and me telling him how I'd win.

When it was all finished, he said I had a good instinct for battles. Too many of the boys from the school choose to commit all their troops forward for a glorious victory without trying to outsmart their opponents. He said that making poor decisions in battle was as dishonourable to a samurai as cheating or cowardice, and he usually had to spend as much time getting his students to think correctly as he spent getting them to fight correctly.

He said he wouldn't usually give anyone a second chance, but he was going to make an exception for me.

He told me to meet him in the garden tomorrow

morning for more training. I thanked him, bowed and left.

GET REAL

Hundreds of castles were built for samurai families in Japan. They were initially used to protect important locations such as trade routes. But they soon developed into elaborate and beautiful structures that showed off how important the families who owned them were. They were often constructed over many different levels with sloping roofs and high towers.

Day Eighteen

When I arrived in the garden this morning I saw that Yoshihiro was clutching his sword. This was more like the training I'd wanted. No

more messing around with pebbles and rice paper. Now it was finally time to jump into slicing up enemies.

The sword was a Katana, just like the one Father has. It has a long, curved blade with a single sharp edge, a grip covered in thick black cloth and a circular guard to stop you getting carried away and slicing off your own fingers instead of your enemy's head.

Yoshihiro held the sword out. I took it and bowed. I was amazed at how light it was for something so big. I put both hands on the grip and leapt into position, with my legs apart and the sword thrust out.

I was hoping Yoshihiro was about to pull out another sword so we could battle, but he just circled me in silence.

He pulled my elbow back and stuck one of my feet forward. He pushed my fingers around the hilt until they were wrapped tightly, even my little fingers, and explained that I needed to keep my grip firm at all times. If an opponent sensed they could break it, they'd send my sword crashing to the ground before sticking theirs into my neck.

I stayed frozen in position while Yoshihiro stared at me. After a while, I asked him when the fighting lesson would begin. He said that today's lesson would not be about battling with the sword. It would be about appreciating it. There was no point in trying to use the sword before I fully understood it.

I was pretty sure I understood what a sword was for, but I let him go on anyway.

He told me about the master swordsmith who had made the weapon, about the rituals of bathing and prayer he went through before creating it, and about the secret art of folding steel into a sharp blade. He told me the blade was alive, and that I needed to spend hours holding it and feeling its power flowing into me before I could fight with it.

I stood perfectly still, willing the ancient magic to flow down the hilt and into my hands. I didn't really feel much, but I wobbled around and blinked anyway to make Yoshihiro think it was happening.

Yoshihiro kept staring at me in silence and nodding occasionally. I found my thoughts drifting to killing enemies, but then worried that Yoshihiro might be able to sense it, so I forced myself to think about the mystic power of the sword again.

My arms began to ache, and my legs began to tremble, but I stayed in position with a look of concentration fixed on my face.

After what seemed like days, Yoshihiro nodded and said I'd done well. Then he said the sword would be mine if I completed his next three tests.

Okay, I can do this. No one will deny that I'm an amazing samurai if I have a sword like that. I need to pass these tests.

GET REAL

The swords used by samurai were carefully forged by craftsmen who were experts in rolling and folding fine strips of steel. They fashioned them into swords such as the katana, which had a long, curved, single-edged blade, and the smaller wakizashi, which was often carried as a backup.

Day Nineteen

I told my brother about the sword Yoshihiro
had promised me, but he just laughed. He said
Yoshihiro had made the same offer to everyone,
and no one had claimed it yet. I think he could
see how much this disappointed me, because he
went on to say it was good that Yoshihiro was
giving me another chance, even if I couldn't win
his sword.

I don't care what he thinks. Just because all the
others failed the tests, it doesn't mean I have
to. I can't wait to see the looks on their faces
when they discover I'm the owner of the sword.

Day Twenty

Every word I'm writing is causing pain. My
wrists are sore and my brush keeps slipping out
of my hand. But I want to get down everything
before I sleep.

I found Yoshihiro on the veranda this morning. He was holding a short metal stick with a round end, and I wondered what sort of weapon it could be.

I followed him into the long room to the left of the main hall, and I immediately realised what was the stick's purpose.

Two gongs had been placed against the walls so they were facing each other. Yoshihiro strolled over to the one on the left and beat it with the hammer. He struck it slowly at first, but went faster until his hand was a blur and the gong was making a continuous low clattering sound.

He said that my test was to copy him exactly. If I was just a tiny fraction out, he'd hear it. But I had all day to try, and I only needed to manage it once.

It didn't sound too bad. With a whole day to practise, I was sure I could learn to keep up.

Yoshihiro pointed to the left side of the room and told me to pick up my beater. At first I couldn't see one, and thought he'd made a mistake. But then I realised what the real challenge was. My beater was very different from his. Rather than being small and made of metal, it was a thin wooden stick that was so long it could barely fit into the room.

I bowed and went over to it. I grabbed the end with both hands and heaved it up, but the wood bent down and the round metal end stayed on the floor.

Yoshihiro stood next to his gong, holding his hammer. He asked me to tell him when I was ready, even though he could clearly see that I was struggling.

I fumbled around with the stick, and finally managed to make it arch up so that the weight was level with the gong. It was awkward and heavy, and my wrists were twisted into a painful position to keep it suspended there.

Yoshihiro began beating his gong, and I tried to follow. But my hands were trembling from the effort of holding the hammer, and I didn't get close to keeping in time.

I dropped my beater to the floor and rubbed my wrists. Yoshihiro just asked me if I was ready to try again.

After a while, the pain died down a little, and I gave it another try.

This time I managed to follow Yoshihiro for the first three strikes before it hurt too much.

I went on like this all morning, waiting for the ache in my arms to die down, then trying again, and failing again.

I could hear the others in the main hall beyond the paper wall. Excited conversation broke out whenever they heard the gong, and I guessed they were remembering their own agonising attempts at the task.

I was sitting on the floor and rubbing my wrists when I had an idea. I didn't know if it would be allowed, but I thought it would be worth trying.

I got up and walked to the far end of the room so I was opposite Yoshihiro. Then I picked up the beater again, but this time I held it at the very front, so my hands were close to the weighted end.

I expected Yoshihiro to tell me to go back, but he just started striking his gong again. I hit mine in perfect time. The rest of the wood was dragging on the floor behind me, so it was still very heavy, but at least it was easier to control.

My arms were throbbing from the effort, but somehow I managed to keep up. I ignored the pain, frantically beating the gong as Yoshihiro sped up, then coming to a complete stop at exactly the same time as him.

Yoshihiro was silent for a few moments. Then he bowed and said I'd passed.

As I strolled out onto the veranda some of the others rushed out of the main hall to see why I'd finished so soon.

My brother asked if I'd given up, but I just casually replied that I'd completed the task and wanted to rest before my next one.

Conversation erupted behind me, and Moriyori had to shout at everyone to get them back inside the hall.

I strolled over to the well to the right of the school, drew a bucket of water and plunged my sore wrists into it.

Day Twenty-One

Yoshihiro woke me at dawn today and led me to the Zen garden. He told me I had until sundown to find the red pebble.

I guessed this was the same pebble he'd sneaked into my hand during the first lesson. But there had to be some more information. I begged him for a clue, and he just said it was very small. I knew that already, so it wasn't much help.

Yoshihiro told me to begin, and walked out.

I paced up and down the path, following it around the pond, past the miniature trees, then around the bushes on the far side.

There must have been thousands of pebbles in it. But I did have a whole day. I probably couldn't check all of them, but I could root through enough to give me a good chance.

I got down on my hands and knees and rifled around. They went down much deeper than I realised, filling a trench that had been dug into the ground. Maybe my chances weren't so good.

I checked the start of the path, the loop at the far end and then some random places in the middle. I saw nothing.

At noon, my brother appeared in the doorway
with a bowl of edamame and some chopsticks. I
thanked him and wolfed it down so I didn't lose
any time.

I asked him where the red stone had been
hidden for other pupils, but he said no one had
ever found it.

I handed the bowl back and got down on my
knees again. I tried to search in a more orderly
way, starting near the entrance and working
my way gradually through every stone.

I'd managed to reach the pool by the time dusk
fell, but there was still no sign of the red pebble
anywhere I looked.

It was getting harder to see any of the pebbles
properly, and I wondered if I'd even know if I
found the red one.

I worked my way forward, passing the miniature trees to my left. I found myself staring at them in the fading light, but couldn't work out why. Then I remembered what Yoshihiro had said. I'd asked him for a clue, and he'd said it was very small. What if this had been about the hiding place rather than the stone?

Please let it be in here...

I crawled over to the first tiny tree and plunged my hand into its soil. There was nothing in it, so I patted it back down. I tried the second one, and still got nothing. Then I tried the third, the smallest of all. I delved into the soil and my hand struck something deep in the pot.

I dragged it out carefully, making sure not to damage the roots.

It was a pebble. It looked darker than all the others, but it was hard to tell in the deepening gloom of the evening.

I got to my feet and raced over to the entrance. I could make out a figure standing there, and I knew from the skinny, upright frame that it was Yoshihiro.

I handed him the pebble and he held it close to his eyes. He glanced over to the horizon, where there was a final slither of orange light.

Yoshihiro nodded and said I'd passed the second test.

Okay. Just one more to go and I will get to keep the sword.

GET REAL

The Japanese art of cultivating miniature versions of trees and shrubs is known as bonsai. Through careful trimming and pruning of leaves and roots, gardeners create perfect replicas of full-grown trees. We know that bonsai was popular in medieval Japan from its many depictions in paintings from the time.

Chapter 4

—

Lessons in combat

Day Twenty-Two

I woke up early this morning, puzzling over what my final task would be. I was imagining something epic or terrifying or impossible. What I wasn't expecting was for Yoshihiro to wait for me to finish eating my seaweed and then tell me to help out with the laundry.

At first I thought it was another of those pathetic jokes that the other pupils were making about me on my first night.

But then Yoshihiro led me to a flat area to the right of the school, and I saw he was serious. Moriyori was watching over ten pupils who were rinsing dirty robes in a wooden tub and beating them against a rock.

Yoshihiro then took me to the well at the side of the school, which was about twenty paces from the pupils. There were two full buckets next to it. He said I had to spend all day carrying the water over to the boys without spilling a drop.

I lugged the heavy buckets up and held them against my chest. I found that I could stagger forward with them resting against me. This wouldn't be easy. But it was possible. The sword was within my grasp.

I set off towards the rocks, but Yoshihiro held out his hand and told me to stop. He said that this was meant to be a test of arm strength. He pulled my arms out until they were fully extended on either side. They soon began to tremble under the effort of holding the water. He said that the test was to carry the water like this all day without spilling a drop.

I stepped forward. The water was so heavy and my arms were so weak that I doubted I could make it to the washing tub once, let alone go back and forth all day.

But then I thought about what he'd said. All I had to do was carry the water all day without spilling a drop. He didn't mention how many trips I had to make. That meant I could go as slowly as I liked.

I edged forward in tiny steps. The water wasn't splashing over the top, but the pain in my arms was unbearable.

A numbness was spreading through my body by the time I was halfway there. I realised I was going to have to run for it before my arms gave way and the buckets fell.

I might spill a drop if I hurried, but I'd definitely spill the whole lot if I didn't.

I started to run. I kept my eyes on the sploshing water in the buckets, so I didn't spot the large stone in front of me.

I caught it with my left foot and fell over. Even as I was keeling forwards, I kept hold of the buckets. I grasped their handles as they slammed to the ground, hoping that all the water might somehow land back inside, and I could get up and continue.

But it sploshed all around me. Moriyori and the boys on laundry duty looked at me and winced.

Yoshihiro was already walking away by the time I got up. So that was it. It was all over. The sword wasn't going to be mine.

Day Twenty—Three

I wondered if failing the last test meant that Yoshihiro was going to give up on me again, but I found him waiting for me this morning in the long room beside the main hall. There were no gongs this time, just two long wooden swords laid out on the mat at the far end.

Yoshihiro offered one to me, and I bowed and accepted it. I grasped the grip with both hands and held it up. It was the same size as a katana, but much heavier.

Yoshihiro said I hadn't won the sword, but he would still give me combat lessons with the wooden bokken.

This cheered me up. I might not have the sword, but at least I was moving on to the next stage of training. No more building up strength and concentration or feeling the ancient power of weapons without actually using them. I was finally going to learn how to kill baddies.

Yoshihiro held his bokken up and asked me to attack. I'd practised for so long with my bamboo stick back in the village, and I couldn't wait to show off my skills.

I swished my bokken forward, and Yoshihiro struck it so violently that it immediately fell to the ground. He told me to keep a stronger grip, and we went again.

This time I lunged forward, hoping to strike
Yoshihiro in the chest, but he stepped aside and
I crashed down onto the mat. He pressed the tip
of his bokken into my neck and said he'd have
been adding to his severed head haul if this
were a real fight.

I imagined my head dangling from the back of a horse. I must remember to put on a brave and defiant expression if anyone ever beheads me. If I'd been killed then, my face would have been forever frozen in an expression of irritation at myself for making such a silly mistake.

I got back up and Yoshihiro told me to keep my legs further apart so I didn't lose my balance. I leapt into a better stance and slashed my bokken forward again. Yoshihiro swept it aside with his. The hard clash sent jolts of pain up my arms, but at least I managed to keep hold of the weapon.

Not that it mattered. In a swift blur of movement, his bokken was at my throat and I was dead again.

It went on like this all day. I'd like to say that I learned from my mistakes, but I didn't. Even if

I'd been that eight-headed dragon Father used to tell me stories about, I'd still have ended up with none.

I crawled back to my sleeping mat covered in bruises and with my hundred imaginary deaths playing in my mind.

GET REAL

The bokken is the name given to a wooden sword used for training samurai. Some were crafted to resemble the long katana, while others stood in for shorter swords like the wakizashi. They were safer for practice than steel swords, but even a bokken could be a lethal weapon in the hands of a skilled fighter.

Day Twenty-Four

Yoshihiro announced that we would have
another day of training with the bokken today
and I was pleased. At first.

I thought that another day of pitting myself
against a master swordsman would be just
what I needed to sharpen my fighting skills.

But it turned out there was a catch. Yoshihiro
wanted me to fight as I would on the field of
battle – in full armour. He pointed to a jumble
of metal and cloth at the far end of the room
and told me to put it on.

I fished some pieces out, pretending I knew
what I was doing. The armour was made from
long plates of iron threaded with tough leather.
I could see how it would stop a sword, but it
was so heavy I doubted I'd be able to get to any
battles with it on.

The arm and leg guards were easy to identify by their shape. I fixed them into place with thick cloth straps.

Next, I found the helmet, which was made from iron strips that hung down in a triangular shape. It was so heavy that I could barely look down to choose my next piece of armour without snapping my neck.

The bit I found next had four wide iron plates held together by a leather belt. I stepped into it and pulled it onto my waist. Yoshihiro didn't complain, so I must have got it right.

There were two further plates of identical size and I guessed these should go over my shoulders, as everything else was pretty much covered by now.

I tied them on and tried to stand up straight. It wasn't easy. The chunks of iron were pressing down on my neck, shoulders and waist, and just staying upright was an effort.

I plodded over to Yoshihiro. It was hard enough trying to walk in the armour. How was I meant to fight in it?

I stopped in front of him, and he bowed. I tried to return the bow, but I think I tilted too far forward. The weight of my helmet and shoulder armour dragged me forward, and I toppled over.

Yoshihiro had to help me back up. I'm pretty

sure a real enemy wouldn't do this, no matter how noble and honest they were.

When I'd settled back on my feet, he handed me my bokken. The combined weight of the wooden sword and the iron armour made it hard to lift my arm at all. Yoshihiro could have been completely unable to move and he'd still have been safe.

I moved my bokken towards him, but he leapt back and then struck out with his. I keeled over backwards, and flailed around like a turtle on its back.

This time he didn't bother to help me up. He just wandered off.

Oh well. So I'm not great at fighting with armour on. Who needs it anyway? I'll just have to get so fast that I can flit around battlefields like a violent shadow, attacking enemies so rapidly that they don't even see me.

GET REAL

Samurai wore suits made of rigid iron panels that were laced or riveted together. Their armour was incredibly heavy, making it difficult for them to run. It was also uncomfortably hot. But it was vital if you wanted to survive a sword attack.

Ordinary soldiers, known as ashigaru, were given armour made of thinner metal. It was easier to move in, but didn't offer the same level of protection.

Day Twenty-Five

Today started with a promising new bit of training and ended in total disaster. Yoshihiro took me to the long room next to the hall and handed me a bow. He said this was the most important weapon of the samurai alongside the sword. It meant you could target enemies on horseback, and from a great distance.

He explained that, as in the first sword lesson, I'd have to get used to handling the bow before I did anything else. I put my serious face back on, in case he asked me to feel its magic power flowing through me.

I got into a wide stance and lifted the bow. It was almost as tall as me, and it was hard to keep it upright as I grabbed the waxy point at the centre of the string and pulled it back.

Yoshihiro made me keep pulling and releasing
the string all morning. I spotted an arrow with
a thin bamboo shaft, white feathers and a sharp
iron head on the floor. I couldn't help my gaze
drifting to it, even though Yoshihiro had said
today would be all about the bow.

But it's not like I'd ever use just the bow in a battle. What was the point of practising without the arrow? I hoped that tomorrow's lesson wouldn't consist of just holding the arrow.

Why did everything have to be so slow? Yoshihiro should just have given me a bow, an arrow and a target and let me fire away. That's how you learn.

Later in the morning, Moriyori appeared at the entrance looking flustered and called Yoshihiro away. I wondered what sort of emergency was going on. I hoped that one of the other pupils had messed up for once instead of me.

When Yoshihiro had gone, I grabbed the arrow. I could dash it to the ground as soon as he came back in, but at that moment I couldn't resist the temptation to try out the weapon properly.

Whooshh

I placed the front of the arrow against the bow, and the back in the tough waxy centre of the string. I stretched it back and forth with the arrow in place. It felt right. Something told me I was going to be good at this.

Maybe I'd finally found my true calling. I would be a great archer, taking out dozens of enemies at long range.

I pulled the string back as far as it would go. Then something terrible happened... I accidentally let go.

The arrow sped forward and ripped through the paper wall into the main hall. I froze and held my breath. I was terrified I'd accidentally impaled one of the other pupils, or maybe even a whole row of them. But I couldn't hear any screaming through the hole.

I let the bow fall to the ground and stepped up to the hole in the wall. Images of injured pupils and angry teachers were running through my mind, but I could never have predicted what I actually saw.

Yoshihiro was standing on the other side, scowling through the hole. Next to him, with his mouth open in shock, was Father.

I yelled that I was sorry and it was an accident, and raced around to see them.

Moriyori and the pupils were gathered at the far side of the hall where the arrow had come to rest. They were staring at me and whispering to each other.

Yoshihiro and my Father were in front of me. I repeated my apologies to Yoshihiro, but he raised his hand to stop me. He said the reason Father had returned early was because they had been called by their daimyo to fight a battle near Kyoto.

I switched my attention to Father and babbled at him about how my training had gone well so far except for this. I told him about how I'd found the red pebble and struck the gong and won the endurance test. I said I was willing to help them fight the battle and promised there would be no more mistakes.

Father said Yoshihiro had already told him I wasn't fit to be a samurai before the arrow had made its surprise appearance.

Yoshihiro added something to explain this, but I couldn't hear it because I was already sobbing so much.

The other pupils gazed at me as tears streamed down my hot cheeks. Most of them were looking down at their feet, but a few were smirking. No doubt these were the idiots who'd assumed I would fail right from the start.

We set off for the village tomorrow. Then Father, Yoshihiro and the five other samurai who live there will quickly report to their daimyo for battle.

I wiped my eyes and stood up straight. My samurai dream was over, but I needed to face my failure with dignity.

But then Father called my brother over and announced that Yoshihiro had declared he was ready to join them. This was so unfair. My brother was going to fight for his lord, while I'd be stuck at home scrubbing the floors.

The tears began to flow again and this time I couldn't stop them.

GET REAL

Daimyo were high-ranking lords who lived on large estates or in impressive castles. They answered only to the shogun, the military leader of Japan.

Samurai would fight for their daimyo in private armies. They were bound by duty to protect their lord and his land. Even if they were hopelessly outnumbered, they would die an honourable death for their masters rather than surrender.

Chapter 5
—
Bandits!

Day Twenty-Eight

I'm home again and the others have gone off to
fight, taking their swords and bows and arrows
with them. If only I could have impressed
Yoshihiro more, I could be out there with them.

The journey back was tough, and my legs
are still aching. Father and Yoshihiro had to
hurry to get everyone ready for battle, and
we only stopped for four hours in the night. I
got through the next day in a dazed state of
exhaustion, with my feet alternating between
pain and numbness.

I spent today trying to convince myself that I
was never meant to be a samurai, but I just
can't. I'm sure I would have been accepted by
Yoshihiro if only I hadn't dropped the buckets.
Or fallen backwards with my armour on. Or
destroyed that wall and nearly killed someone.

Day Twenty-Nine

I strolled around the village today telling everyone about my training. I mainly focused on the tasks I did well on rather than the ones that I had failed.

They're probably wondering why Father didn't take me to battle with him if I'd been so good.

I bet Yoshihiro and my father and brother are already fighting. They're probably comparing severed head collections while I'm stuck here with only old people and children to hear my tales of heroism.

GET REAL

Collecting the severed heads of enemies was a common practice for samurai. They would tie the heads to their horses and take them back for their lords to see. The hair on the heads would sometimes be neatly arranged before the lord inspected it, and make-up could even be applied to the dead faces.

Day Thirty

Mother made me help her with the laundry this afternoon. As well as being tedious, it also reminded me of my failure at Yoshihiro's test. As soon as Mother went off to get more water, I ran into our sleeping room.

At the end of Father's mat was a large roll of cloth tied with cord. I knew he kept his swords in there, but I wasn't sure if he'd left any behind.

I picked it up. There was something inside. This was promising.

I unrolled it. There was a bokken, a bow with a broken string and a wooden sheath. I unrolled the last piece and gasped. There was a katana in there. It was rusty and blunt, and must have been the one Father used when he was young. But it was a samurai sword all the same, and I could continue my training with it.

I knew Mother wouldn't be happy if she saw me using it, so I carried it out to the jagged rocks.

I leapt about with the blunt katana, trying to remember my bokken training. I imagined

Yoshihiro was in front of me and failing to block any of my moves. He was saying I was now a master sword fighter and that he wouldn't hesitate to take me along to the next battle.

Yoshihiro's imaginary voice was soon drowned out by two real voices. I looked down at the path. Two men were climbing towards me.

I lowered my sword and crouched behind one of the rocks so I could spy on them. The men were both wearing torn, dirty robes and had scruffy beards and moustaches. One was tall with thin, wispy hair that was greying at the sides and the other was short with thick black hair and eyebrows that met in the middle. They were both carrying wooden lances with very sharp iron tips.

They were pointing towards the village as they walked, but I couldn't make out what they were saying. I stayed totally still as they approached and tried to breathe as quietly as I could.

As they got nearer, I could hear snatches of their conversation. The older one was saying the village must be unprotected because they'd seen so many samurai walking away from it, so they could just take what they wanted. The younger one warned him not to steal anything yet. They were only here to check the samurai were really gone.

I felt my heart pounding. My rusty sword trembled in my hands. The men were bandits, and they were here to attack us.

I wondered if I could race back and warn the others. Together we'd outnumber them, and we'd surely have a chance. But there wasn't time.

There was only one way to get rid of them. I was going to have to scare them off.

I ran through the narrow gap between the rocks and stopped on the other side. I got into the stance Yoshihiro had shown me, with my legs apart and the tip of my sword at neck level.

The men came to a halt and put pitiful expressions on their faces. The younger man said they were poor beggars who wanted nothing but a little rice and water and then they'd be on their way.

I told them they weren't beggars. They were bandits. And they wanted to attack our village because they thought all the samurai had gone. But they were wrong. I was a mighty samurai warrior and I would chop both their heads off in one swoop if they took another step forward.

The men looked at each other in confusion. I'd have preferred it if they had looked terrified, but at least they weren't running forward with their lances raised.

I held my ground and managed not to shake or whimper. If the bandits came any closer they'd see how old and rusty my sword was, and they'd know I wasn't telling the truth. Then they'd charge at me and realise I wasn't as good a fighter as I'd been claiming.

But they stayed exactly where they were as I stared at them with the fiercest, scariest gaze I could manage.

Eventually the older man lowered his lance and turned away. He walked back down the path, and the younger man followed him.

I stood in the narrow pass and watched them until they were out of sight. Then I rushed back to the village to tell everyone who would listen about my brilliant victory.

Mother was one of the first people I saw, and she began to scold me for abandoning the laundry. But she soon stopped when I told her I'd just foiled an enemy attack.

I rang the bell in the middle of the village until everyone had emerged from their houses.

Soon I was standing in front of a crowd of children, old people and the samurai's wives. I told them how I'd frightened away the bandits. I even drew out my sword to illustrate it, which made some of the smaller children flinch back.

I reached the part where the bandits fled and waited for the others to thank me. It didn't happen though.

Kuroki and his wife Akemi wailed that the bandits were coming for us, which wasn't the reaction I'd been hoping for.

I asked if they'd even been listening. I'd just got
rid of the invaders. We should be celebrating,
not crying.

Kuroki sighed and shook his head. He said the village had been raided by bandits before, and they never give up. The two men hadn't been planning to attack today, they just wanted to check there were no samurai left before returning with a bigger group.

Akemi wailed even louder and said there was no one to protect us.

It was typical of Kuroki to bring the mood down like that, though I supposed he was right. But I couldn't agree with what Akemi had said.

I said that they did have someone to protect them, and that person was me. I pretended Yoshihiro had said I was a great samurai and ready to battle at the highest level. This was a slight exaggeration. Or rather, a complete lie.

But what was I meant to do? We had to fight back instead of cowering in our homes and waiting for the bandits to steal all our stuff.

And to battle back, the villagers would need someone strong to follow. And even if I'd only had a few days of samurai training, it was more than all the others put together.

I raised my sword in the air and asked who was with me. The only reply I got was a low sobbing from Akemi.

GET REAL

The sword and the bow were the most important weapons in medieval Japan. Although some guns were introduced in the 16th century, they weren't seen as reliable weapons at first. A skilled archer could shoot many arrows in the time it took to load and fire a gun. But these new weapons eventually became more efficient and were adopted by samurai.

Day Thirty-One

No sign of the bandits so far. I hope they hold off for at least a few more days. I intend to turn the terrified inhabitants of this village into an army, and I'll need all the time I can get.

I woke up early this morning and gathered long strips of bamboo that could stand in for swords.

123

Then I rang the bell and made everyone line up
on the flat ground in front of it. I handed out
the sticks and announced it was time to learn
sword-fighting.

I demonstrated the correct way to stand and
grip, just as Yoshihiro had shown me. I tried to

remember all I could of the speech about how the sword should become an extension of your arm and how you should feel its ancient power running into your body.

They looked confused, so I moved on to miming some basic fighting moves.

I struck out with my sword, pressing it to the throat of an imaginary opponent. They did this too. Then I swung it to the side, as if blocking an attack. They did this too. Then I tried to lunge forward, but overbalanced and got the tip of my sword stuck in the ground. They copied this too.

I explained that they weren't meant to have fallen over too, and ran through the sequence again. This time I got it right, but an old woman accidentally hit her husband on the back of the head with her sword, and a genuine fight broke out between two of the children.

Kuroki asked why I was giving them sword-fighting lessons if we didn't have any actual swords for them to fight with.

Once again, he was bringing everyone down when I was trying to get them excited. And once again, he was right.

I told them to spend the rest of the day searching for anything that could be used as a weapon, and we'd resume the lesson tomorrow when we knew what we had to work with.

Day Thirty-Two

I rang the bell early this morning and got everyone to place their weapons on the ground. In addition to the bokken and broken bow, there were three knives, a smaller wooden sword, three arrows, an axe, a chisel, a rake and a broom.

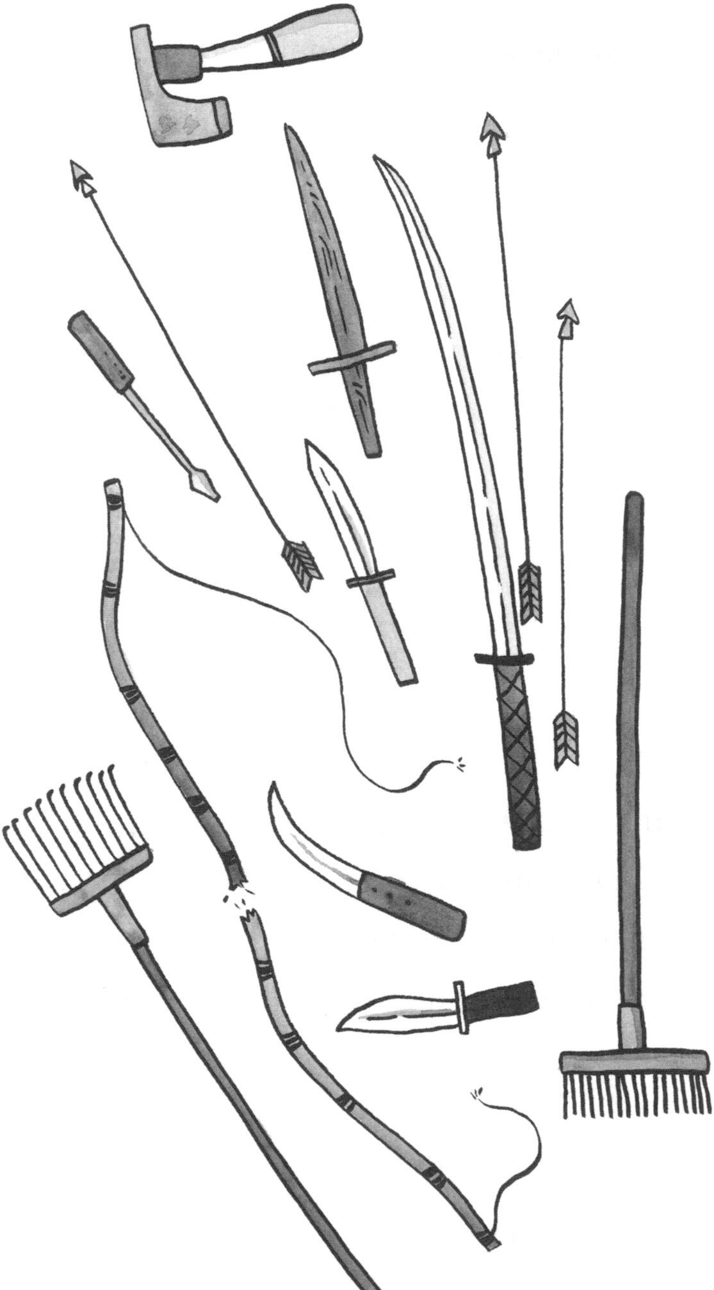

I sighed. We'd struggle to kill a fish with that lot, never mind a pack of reckless bandits.

Everyone was looking at me to explain how we were going to defeat the invaders with this bizarre assortment of weapons and I had no idea. But they were counting on me, and I needed to act like I knew.

I remembered the tactics lesson Yoshihiro had given me, and I used the bokken to sketch out a map of our village in the dirt. Everyone crowded around to look at it.

There were four ways the bandits could approach us. The first was up the main path that led through the jagged rocks. The second was down the high cliffs at the back of the village. And the third and fourth were through the forests on either side.

The map looked a lot like the first one Yoshihiro had drawn in his tactics lesson. We didn't have a castle to hide in, but that didn't mean I couldn't defend our village in a similar way.

I said we'd need to chop down the trees at the front of both forests. Then we should dig pits in front of them, and stick sharp shards of wood in the bottom. I marked out deep lines in the sand to show exactly where the trenches should go.

I told Fujioka to take charge of this, and he nodded silently.

Then I thought about the steep cliffs at the back of the village. The bandits might try and come down that way, but it would be hard for them to find a path if they'd never been there before. We'd spot them approaching, and we could climb up to the higher ledges and pelt them with stones.

Most of the children were too young to help,
but there were six who were just a few years
younger than me. I told them to gather rocks
and hide them on ledges, then practise getting
up and down quickly.

Then there was the main path. The bandits
would have better weapons than us, but they'd
need to get through the narrow pass. We'd have
to defend it from our side with our knives, axes
and brooms.

I tried to mark out the route the thieves would
take with arrows, but I made a mess of it and
had to scrub it out. Fujioka nodded again, as
though he understood what it all meant.

Next I marked out a spot on top of the rocks
and told the samurai wives to carry the village
bell there and take turns watching the path day
and night. They were to ring the bell as soon as

they saw anyone approach, and we'd all have to sleep with our weapons at our sides, so we were ready to run out if we heard it.

I told the old people to keep watch on the forests and I told the children to keep watch on the cliffs.

I turned to Takenaka, who carved some impressive wooden figures for me when I was little. I asked if she knew how to mend a broken bow, and she said she'd try her best.

I was feeling pretty good now I had a plan, and I launched into a speech about how we might not be samurai, but we could fight as well as the mightiest warrior if we needed to.

A few of the children cheered, but then Kuroki and Akemi ruined everything by saying we were all going to be slain by the bandits. I gave them the night watch as a punishment.

Day Thirty-Three

I spent this morning rubbing my sword against a rock to sharpen it. I checked it and immediately wished I hadn't. I winced as a thick red blob of blood trickled down my finger.

The sword was still rusty and slightly bent, but it would do the job when the bandits came.

Then I wandered around the village to see how my troops were doing. Fujioka was proving surprisingly strong, and had already managed to create a thick barrier of fallen trees to the east of the village. Two of the other old people were helping him dig a wide trench in front of it.

Over on the cliffs, the children were scurrying up to the ledges and dropping stones off. I had to drag some of the smaller onlookers back to make sure none were accidentally squashed.

Then I checked the main path. The bell and its wooden stand had been lugged to the top of the jagged rocks and Mother was on lookout duty.

I clambered up and greeted her. I thought she might be annoyed that I'd taken command of the village and neglected my chores, but she said I was doing a good job.

Everyone seems to have accepted me as leader now, even Mother. I just hope I don't let them down when the time comes.

Day Thirty–Four

I gathered all the samurai wives for combat training today. They lined up and I handed out the weapons we'd managed to gather. The ones I came to first got knives and bokken, but the ones at the end had to make do with rakes and brooms.

In truth, none of the weapons were likely to do much damage, but maybe if we worked together we could get the better of the villains.

I paced down the line telling one woman that the knife was an extension of her body, telling another the chisel was an extension of her body, and another that the broom was an extension of her body. I couldn't bring myself to tell them to feel ancient power flowing through them. It's not what you want to hear when you're having to defend yourself with a soup ladle.

I got them to adopt a fighting stance and hold their weapons as if they were deadly swords. Then I taught them to thrust them up to throat level, to use them to block their enemies, and to swing them round to surprise their opponents with a side attack. Though I expect their opponents would already be pretty surprised if they were being attacked with a rake.

136

We kept practising all day, and soon I had transformed a group of dutiful wives into a fearsome, merciless army.

Well, almost. But at least we'll be able to put up a much better fight now.

Day Thirty-Five

I was patrolling our defences when Takenaka approached and offered me Father's bow. She'd managed to reattach the strings, and rub wax along them. It looked thinner than the one Yoshihiro had given me, but felt just as strong when I pulled it.

I thanked Takenaka and raced home to collect the arrows. I was so pleased to have another weapon that I almost forgot I'd only ever fired one arrow, and that it had accidentally destroyed a wall.

I needed to practise, but it wouldn't be good for morale if everyone saw how awful I was.

I remembered a clearing in the east woods where Yasutaro and I used to go and play samurai when we were little. I hadn't gone there for a while, but I could remember every step of the path we'd worked out through the dense cypress trees.

I headed over to it. Fujioka was busy digging the trench in front of the forest, and didn't see me slip past.

I made it to the open space and scratched out a mark on one of the tree trunks. This could be the throat of one of the bandits.

I stepped over to the far side of the clearing, raised my bow, pulled the arrow back, and then let it go.

It sailed through the air, missing the tree altogether, and got lost in a tangle of dry branches. When I'd finally managed to retrieve it, I tried again. And missed again.

Each time I attempted another shot, I took a step closer. By the time I actually hit the target, I was so close I might as well have used my sword.

I stopped. I could hear something deep in the woods. A sort of low crunching. It could have just been a falling branch, but it might also have been a bandit.

I found myself grabbing my arrows and running away. I didn't quite know why. If an invader was coming, surely I should have taken cover and picked them off with my arrows? But I wasn't feeling too confident about my archery skills after such a terrible day of training.

My feet picked out the winding path they'd traced a hundred times before. I should have slowed down as I approached the edge of the forest, but I was still convinced a bandit was coming after me. Instead, I burst through the thin gap between two trees, and ended up falling right into Fujioka's trench.

I tried to scrabble out before he could find me, but it was too deep and the sides were extremely slippery.

140

Fujioka soon appeared and looked down at me in confusion. I held out my hand and he yanked me out. Wiping the mud from my robe, I told him he'd done very well, and the trench had passed my inspection.

He said I should have warned him I was going to test it, as he was just about to fix the shards of wood in the bottom. Ouch. That would have hurt a lot.

Now I'm back home and reflecting on my day. I learned that I'm not very good at shooting arrows, that I'll probably turn and run if I hear anyone coming, and that I'm just as likely to fall into the traps as the bandits. So overall, I'm not feeling great about my chances of defending the village.

Chapter 6

Caught!

Day Thirty–Six

I heard a cry coming from the direction of the west forest this morning, and I raced over. I hoped Fujioka hadn't fallen into the trench too.

I hurtled through the rice field and the edge of the trees came into view. Fujioka was staring down into the pit, so at least he was alright.

I ran over to him and looked down into the trench. The older bandit was crouching at the bottom. One of the shards of wood had pierced his foot and he was trying to pull it out. His hands were covered in blood and splinters, and he was weeping with pain.

His lance had fallen a little further along, just out of his reach.

It was great that my plan had worked, and we'd captured one of the thieves. But I didn't feel much like celebrating as I stared at his sobbing face and bleeding foot.

I told myself to be merciless. I needed to shoot an arrow into his heart, then fetch my sword and begin my severed head collection. But the man looked so pathetic and desperate as he cowered at the bottom of the trench.

Others from the village were gathering to see what was going on, but I told them to get back to their posts. This could be just the start of a co-ordinated attack.

They wandered away and I got ready to kill the bandit. I placed one of the arrows into the bow and aimed it at him.

He wept and pleaded with me not to kill him. I forced myself to ignore him and got ready to release the arrow.

146

Another loud scream rang out. This time it came from the cliffs at the back of the village.

I handed the bow and arrow to Fujioka and told him to keep guard. Then I ran back through the rice fields and made my way over to the cliffs. When I got there, I saw the younger bandit had arrived too.

He was rolling around on the ground at the bottom of the cliff, while the children pelted him with stones. He was cradling his right hand, and his lance had fallen a few paces away.

I grabbed it and pointed it at him.

I told the children to stop throwing rocks and asked him if others were coming. He said they weren't. The two of them had only come to spy and check that the samurai had really abandoned the village.

I told him he was looking at a samurai right now, and it would be the last thing he'd ever see. I felt quite pleased with myself for sounding so harsh.

Some of the children gasped and gathered around the bandit to watch his execution.

I raised the sharp tip of the lance up to the bandit's throat. He begged for his life even more desperately than his friend had done.

I told myself to press it in. My severed head collection could go from none to two in a single day. But how much did I really want a severed head collection anyway? I'd only remember the pitiful pleading of the bandits every time I looked at their rotting skulls.

Oh, go on. Just a little bit of head-chopping?

I told the bandit to get up and walk ahead of me. He thanked me for sparing him, and the children groaned in disappointment.

I marched him through the rice field and over to the pit with his friend in it.

Fujioka pulled the older bandit out and we walked them both back to the main path. I kept the lance pressed into the younger one's back, and Fujioka kept the arrow pointed at the older one's head.

The older bandit could only hop, and had to rest his arm around his friend's neck. Some of the children gathered behind us and shouted insults at the pathetic thieves.

When we reached the narrow pass between the jagged rocks, I told the men they could go if they promised never to return. They agreed, thanked me and wiped the tears from their eyes.

We clambered up onto the rocks and watched them hobble away. When they were out of earshot, Fujioka confessed that he had no idea how to use the bow and arrow. I whispered that I didn't either, really.

150

I hope I don't regret letting the bandits go. If we could have stuck their heads on poles on top of the rocks, it would have sent out a message to anyone else thinking of coming. But I just couldn't bring myself to kill them when they were crying in front of me. It's easy to murder imaginary enemies, but harder to do it when they're real people standing in front of you and staring at you with their red, tearful eyes.

GET REAL

Some samurai were ruthless killers, but others saw mercy as part of their code of honour. They believed fierce warriors should use their power for good, and deadly combat skills should be learned only by those who could show sympathy and pity.

Day Thirty—Seven

No sign of any more bandits. I don't believe
the two I let go will really stay away, but they
might be taking some time to recover before
they come back with a larger group.

They'll know our samurai are away now, but
they'll also know that they can't come down the
cliffs or go through the forest.

When they arrive, it will be on the main path,
and that's where we must focus now. I'll stand
on top of the jagged rocks and fire my arrows at
them as they walk along it.

The others can wait behind the narrow pass
with their knives, rakes and brooms. We might
not stand much of a chance against their
swords, but at least we'll die with honour.

152

When Father and the others return, they'll see we faced danger like true warriors instead of running away and cowering.

GET REAL

Courage was an important part of the samurai code. Running away from battle, even if you were facing certain defeat, would bring shame to you and your family.

Day Thirty-Eight

Still no sign of them. I have chosen Mother and Takenaka to wield the lances we took from the first bandits, and today I gave them some training. Or at least, I tried to. Yoshihiro never gave me any lance lessons, but I did my best to sound like I knew what I was talking about.

I told them to stand up straight and hold the tips of the lances to the throats of their imaginary opponents. Then we practised pulling the lances back and thrusting them forward to deliver a killing blow.

Takenaka managed to follow my instructions perfectly. But Mother couldn't stay in time, and I kept having to stop and make her do it again. After all those years of being told I was doing my chores wrong, it was fun to finally turn the tables on her.

Surprisingly, Mother didn't even argue back. She's accepted that I'm in charge now, just like everyone else.

I'd feel pretty good about it if it wasn't for the group of bloodthirsty bandits waiting to invade.

Ring

Day Thirty-Nine

It was still dark this morning when I was woken by the bell. I grabbed my sword, bow and arrows and ran over to the rocks. The others were already gathering, so I pushed through and climbed to the top of the jagged rocks.

Takenaka was on guard duty, and she'd spotted movement in the far distance. It was hard to make anything out, and at first I thought she might have woken us all for no good reason. But as I peered into the gloom, I found I could make out eight figures moving slowly towards us.

I told everyone to get into position and wait for my instructions. It was time to fight.

Mother and Takenaka stood behind the narrow pass, and held their lances out to block it. The samurai wives gathered behind them, ready to pounce on anyone who got through.

I climbed onto the highest rock and placed my first arrow into my bow.

Okay, so there were eight bandits. This was going to be tough. But I could reduce their number to five if I scored a fatal hit with each of my arrows.

As the group got closer, I could see that the two figures at the back were limping slightly, and one was much taller than the other. Our old friends were back, despite their promises to keep away.

I aimed my arrow at the tall bandit and stretched the bow back. I let it go. It plummeted straight down, landing nowhere near any of the invading bandits.

I knew I should be taking time to think. Shooting over such a long range would be difficult for the most skilled archer. For someone who couldn't even hit a tree they were standing right next to, it would be impossible.

I tried to make myself wait until the group got closer and give myself at least a small chance of hitting them. But I'd given in to my anger. They'd gone back on their word and now I wanted revenge.

I picked up the second arrow and placed it in the bow. This time I aimed for the air above the tall bandit, hoping that the arrow would arc down onto his head.

The arrow flew high, but it was too steep. It rose up then fell straight down again, landing closer to us than them.

Without pausing, I fired off my last arrow. This time it hurtled along, not too high and not too low. I followed its white feathers as it sped towards the group.

I sighed. The arrow landed on the ground in front of the tall bandit.

Not only had I wasted my last chance, but I'd drawn their attention. The tall bandit pointed at me and shouted something at the others. Then they all held out their swords and ran up the hill towards me.

I told everyone to get ready to fight. I did my best to sound confident, but my voice was already wavering.

The six new bandits looked much stronger and fiercer than the ones we'd already met. And I'd managed to take out absolutely none of them with my arrows. This was going to be a fierce, bloody battle.

I held my sword up as they stormed towards us. I wanted to look like a fearsome warrior and

160

frighten them off, but it's not easy when your legs are shaking.

I shut my eyes and told myself to be brave. I had a sword. I'd trained with a master samurai, even though it hadn't gone very well. I still had a chance.

When I opened my eyes, I saw that something very strange had happened. The bandits had suddenly disappeared.

I glanced down at the bottom of the rocks to see if they'd somehow managed to make it all the way there already, but there was no sign of them anywhere.

It was like one of those moments when you put your cup or writing brush down, and then when you look again it's gone. Except the missing thing in this case was eight merciless robbers.

I heard screams coming from a dark patch further down the hill. I could just about make out a narrow gap, as if the hill had cracked open without warning.

Takenaka asked if they were close yet, and I replied that I couldn't actually see them. I tried my best not to sound too confused.

Fujioka said they must have fallen right into the trench. He said he'd made it very deep, just like I'd wanted.

At first I had no idea what he was talking about. But then I thought back to the day I'd drawn my map in the sand. I made a mess of it by trying to draw arrows at the front and then crossing them out. Fujioka must have thought I was asking for another trench halfway down the hill, cutting across the path.

I'd have thought the ground there would be too hard and rocky to dig in, but it looked like Fujioka had managed it.

I thanked him for carrying out my plan and scrambled down from the rocks. I walked slowly down to the trench and the others followed.

As we approached, I got Mother and Takenaka to flank me on either side with the lances in case any of the thieves decided to leap up and attack us.

The first streaks of light were appearing in the sky as I peered down into the pit. All eight of the bandits were at the bottom, wincing and picking shards of wood out of their feet and legs.

They were covered in moss, rocks and twigs, the remains of a false covering Fujioka must have laid over the trench.

The bandits, who had looked so fierce a few moments ago, now seemed totally helpless. I should have put an end to it all by burying them alive, but I couldn't bring myself to do it.

I told them I'd let them go if they handed their weapons over and agreed to stay away forever. Murmurs of agreement came from the trench.

Seven swords, some of which were as old and rusty as mine, landed on the ground in front of us. I handed them to the samurai wives.

Then I lowered the broom into the deep hole and used it to pull the bandits up one by one. None of them tried to fight when they were out. They just jumped back across the gap and slouched away down the hill.

Soon they were all wandering away with their heads bowed and their shoulders slumped. The tall bandit who'd visited the other day seemed to have twisted his ankle, and was limping far behind the others and asking them to wait.

The Sun came up as we watched them hobble away out of sight. Then we made our way back to the village.

Everyone congratulated me on my great plan, and I didn't have the heart to admit it had been an accident.

Takenaka said I was a brilliant leader and it was no wonder my teacher had said I was ready to be a samurai. I'd almost forgotten about that lie. I'll have a lot of explaining to do when Father hears about it.

Day Forty

Maybe I should have killed the bandits when I had the chance. The first two didn't keep their promise to stay away, so there's no reason they will this time. But at least we have better weapons now, I suppose.

I let the others get back to their normal lives today, but I stayed on the rocks with my sword in my hand, looking out for movement.

I saw nothing, but I can't get rid of the feeling that the threat isn't over yet.

Chapter 7

A great samurai

Day Forty-One

I couldn't sleep last night, so I grabbed my sword and made for the jagged rocks again. I stood on the top, gazing down the path.

It was too dark to see properly, but I thought I could see something in the far distance.

I wondered if I was imagining it. After all, I'd been staring at the path for so long, and I'd had so little sleep, that I couldn't trust my eyes.

I scrabbled over to the bell, but couldn't bring myself to ring it. I was a hero to everyone in the village, but if I woke them up in the middle of the night for a false alarm that would all change immediately.

I went back to the high rock and stared down at the path. I'd been right. There were definitely people approaching.

I could make out eight figures. The bandits were back. And they must have all recovered quickly from their injuries because they were hurrying towards me.

There was no time to think about it. I'd already waited too long. I dashed over to the bell and rang it.

I could hear distant cries from the village, but no footsteps. It was going to take a while for the others to wake up. Meanwhile, the bandits were gaining fast, and there was only me to fend them off.

Fighting eight reckless thieves with their hearts set on revenge was going to be tough, even if they didn't have swords. But I couldn't live with the dishonour of running away. Yoshihiro might not have wanted me to be a samurai, but at least I could die like one.

I lifted my sword and ran down the path screaming at the bandits.

I screamed louder and blinked tears from my eyes as I got closer. They seemed to be shouting something, but I couldn't hear or see them very well in the dark.

I charged at them with my sword out. The one at the front had a sword too. This wasn't good. They must have found some other weapons to attack us with.

The bandit clashed his sword into mine with such force that I tumbled to the ground and my weapon rolled away.

So this was it. I would be an easy kill for the bandits now. I just hoped they'd make it quick.

But none attacked. Instead, they seemed to be calling my name. How did they know it?

I wiped the tears from my eyes and looked up. Yoshihiro and Father were looking down at me. Behind them was my brother and the five others who had gone to battle.

Yoshihiro tucked his sword back into his belt and asked what I was doing. I tried to tell him about the bandits, but I knew I wasn't making sense. The fall had knocked the wind out of me and a wave of exhaustion was hitting.

Yoshihiro pulled me to my feet and we continued up the path. By now the others from the village were streaming down to meet them.

Soon excited conversations were breaking out all around me. The samurai were telling their families about their victory in battle, and the families were telling them about our brave defence of the village.

As we reached our house, Father caught up with me and said he'd heard all about the brilliant work I'd done while they were away. He wanted me to tell him more, but I said I needed to sleep first.

All the worry that had been surging through me had gone, and I could barely keep my eyes open.

Day Forty—Two

The bell is back in the centre of the village now. We gathered around it this afternoon and Father made me tell the story of how we protected the village. I told him every detail, except that I hadn't actually meant for Fujioka to dig the big trench. Father said he was very proud of me, and congratulated the others for carrying out my plan so well.

There was something I still needed to apologise for, and I thought I should do it while Father would be in a forgiving mood. I admitted that I'd pretended Yoshihiro had said I was a great samurai. I knew this was a lie, but I thought it would be easier for the village to rally around a brilliant fighter than someone who had failed their training.

Father said he understood, and that I was completely forgiven.

Then Yoshihiro stepped forward and said there was nothing to forgive because it wasn't a lie. Now that he'd heard how I'd protected the village, he really did think I was a great samurai. He asked me to return to school with him so I could complete my training.

I agreed at once, even though I knew I was letting myself in for a world of frustration and pain. But I know it will all be worth it, because I'll emerge as a brilliant warrior.

Then Yoshihiro offered his sword to me with both hands. He said he'd finally found a pupil worthy of it.

I bowed and took it. Then I stepped back and held it up. Now I could understand everything he'd said about the sword being part of me, and about its ancient power. I'd tried so hard to feel like this during training, but now it was happening naturally.

With my new sword in my hands, I could see a future of tough battles and glorious victories laid out before me.

All my life I've felt like I was destined to become a great warrior. It turns out I was right.

The End

Samurai warriors

Samurai were a fierce group of Japanese warriors who were at their most important between the 12th and 18th centuries. They served lords known as daimyo, who owned land and were in charge of private armies.

Much of the samurai era was marked by fierce conflict between feuding clans. Rivals would fight each other in violent battles that lasted for months or years. They would have to survive in a harsh rocky landscape, braving heavy rain in summer and snow in winter.

They followed a code known as Bushido, which required honesty, courage and absolute loyalty to their lords. They would fight to the death to defend their daimyo, and seek revenge on anyone who wronged them. Going to battle was seen as a male duty, though women were expected to defend their homes from attack. However, a number of female samurai such as Tomoe Gozen became legendary warriors and commanders.

The era of civil war came to an end in the
early 17th century following the victory of
Tokugawa Ieyasu in the battle of Sekigahara.
A period of peace followed, and samurai
began to learn about philosophy and the arts
as well as military skills. Edo, now known as
Tokyo, was the centre of power for this time,
so it is often called the Edo period.

In 1868 the last of the shoguns descended
from Tokugawa was overthrown, and Japan
was opened to international trade. Industry
and business were the important things in
this new world, and the samurai seemed to
belong to the distant past.

But the idea of the samurai remained a part of Japanese identity. Popular martial arts such as judo, kendo and karate require the strength and self-control of the great warriors. Learning them will give you a taste of the tough training that young samurai had to endure.

The samurai lives on in countless games, anime, manga and movies. The filmmaker Akira Kurosawa directed many classic films about them, including *Ran*, *Throne of Blood* and *Seven Samurai*.

And the samurai code of duty, loyalty and honesty continues to inspire Japanese people in all walks of life.

Samurai castles

The period 1570–1690 is often called the
'Golden Age' of Japanese castle building.
Unlike traditional Japanese buildings, they
were several storeys high. 'Golden Age'
castles were also admired for their innovative
layout. They were planned as clusters of
towers, and included features like gateways,
courtyards and reception halls, borrowed
from all kinds of traditional buildings, from
temples to townhouses.

The resulting castles were very beautiful,
with carved and painted woodwork and steep,
soaring roofs. The outer walls of Matsue
castle (completed 1611) were covered in
shiny black lacquer, earning it the nickname
'Raven Castle'. Hikone castle (completed

1603) was decorated in gold. Himeji castle (completed 1609) was covered in special, fireproof white plaster. This, plus its graceful, curving gables, won it the name 'White Egret Castle'. Until the early 17th century, these magnificent castles had an extra purpose: to display samurai power. That is why, in 1615, shogun Ieyasu banned samurai from building more than one castle on each of their estates.

Originally, strength and security were the prime consideration for samurai, but soon castle interiors began to be planned – at least in part – as showcases for their owner's wealth, good breeding and excellent taste.

How do we know about samurai warriors?

The era of the great samurai began over eight hundred years ago. So how do we know so much about it?

One reason is that many written documents have survived. There are hundreds of scrolls, letters and maps that give us valuable evidence about the world of the samurai.

Finely crafted pieces of art have also survived. These include paintings, sculptures, pottery and carvings. Other objects can teach us about Japanese life. Many genuine swords still exist, some dating back to the very beginning of the samurai period.

Buildings such as castles, Buddhist temples and Shinto shrines are still standing. Millions of tourists every year visit Himeji Castle, which was rebuilt in 1609.

And some research is more gruesome. Scientists have examined the skeletons of samurai to find out things like how they were killed and how many had their heads chopped off to become battle trophies.

Timeline

1192 AD

Minamoto Yoritomo becomes shogun for life after winning the Genpei War. It ushers in an era in which samurai become powerful figures.

1336 AD

Ashikaga Takauji defeats Emperor Go-Daigo and becomes shogun. The Muromachi period begins, named after the district of Kyoto where the government was based.

1467 AD

The Ōnin War marks the beginning of the 'Age of Warring States'. This was a long period of violent conflict in which powerful daimyo and their armies fought for dominance.

Timeline

1543 AD

Portuguese traders arrive in Japan for the first time. Over the next few years traders will introduce goods that will transform samurai life, such as muskets, which are heavy guns that are fired from the shoulder.

1603 AD

Tokugawa Ieyasu becomes shogun, having defeated his rival warlords and seized power. He passes strict laws to stop the violent feuding between daimyos and their armies. The 'Edo period' of Japan begins.

Timeline

1609 AD

Himeji Castle is rebuilt into a stunning complex with multiple levels, steep roofs and walls covered in white plaster. This is the golden age of castle building, when daimyo were competing to build extravagant structures that would display their power.

1853 AD

Commodore Matthew Perry arrives in Edo Bay with a fleet of American ships, demanding trade with Japan. Many are worried that Japan has fallen behind other nations in areas like technology and military power, and they argue that it must change.

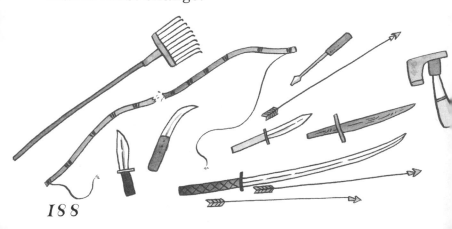

Timeline

1867 AD

Tokugawa Yoshinobu resigns, marking the end of a dynasty founded over 250 years earlier by Tokugawa Ieyasu.

1868 AD

Emperor Meiji takes control of Japan and sets about transforming the country into a modern industrial nation. The time of the samurai is finally over.

1954 AD

Akira Kurosawa's classic film *Seven Samurai* is released. The samurai are long gone, but they live on in the imaginations of many great artists and storytellers.

Samurai Hall of Fame

Hangaku Gozen (c. 12th century)

Female warrior who fought as an ally of the Taira clan in the Genpei War. She is said to have commanded an army of 3,000 soldiers. After her death, she became a popular figure in paintings and prints, and is often shown wielding the naginata, which is a long wooden pole with a curved blade on the end.

Kusunoki Masashige (1294–1336 AD)

Most samurais were loyal only to their own families. Kusunoki Masashige became famous for his support of Emperor Go-Daigo, who came to power in 1318. Go-Daigo was one of the few Japanese emperors who wanted to stand up to the shoguns and rule for himself. Kusunoki Masashige gave him wise advice, but he was overruled by courtiers, who had none of his samurai skills. However, he chose to loyally obey the emperor's orders, and was eventually killed in battle.

Samurai Hall of Fame

Minamoto Tametomo (1139–1170 AD)

Legendary samurai archer. He was said to have won many battles with his bow skills, and it's even claimed that he once sunk an entire ship by firing an arrow into its hull. His amazing skills were apparently down to his right arm being much longer than his left arm, giving him more pull on the bowstring.

Minamoto Yoritomo (1147–1199 AD)

Ruthless leader who had his brother and cousins put to death on his rise to power. He defeated the Taira clan in the Genpei war, then placed allies in provinces all around Japan and made them lords. He now had power over the whole country, and in 1192 he became Shogun for life. He was fierce enough to win battles and wise enough to hold onto power.

Samurai Hall of Fame

Oda Nobunaga (1534–1582 AD)

Warrior and military leader who was known for his brilliant battle tactics. He once defeated a much larger army by making his troops circle them and launch a surprise attack, and was the first samurai lord to equip his troops with muskets as well as swords. He conquered many provinces and brought them together under his rule, laying the groundwork for the unification of Japan and an end to the age of warring states.

Otomo Yakamochi (718–785 AD)

Otomo Yakamochi lived in the 8th century. Although not a very effective warrior – the Emperor Kanmu called him an 'incompetent coward' – he was the first warrior to receive the title of shogun.

Samurai Hall of Fame

The Soga family

The Soga family were rich, noble warriors with friends – and enemies – at the emperor's court. They wanted to 'modernise' the way Japan was governed by introducing new ideas borrowed from China. But other noble families disagreed. So, in AD 587, Soga warriors fought a battle at Shigisen, and won. In 592, one of the family, Prince Shōtoku, became emperor. He passed many new laws, transforming the way the country was run.

Samurai Hall of Fame

Taira family

The Taira family were the most powerful
samurai in 12th-century Japan; they ruled
on behalf of the 8-year-old emperor Antoku.
But they were defeated at the sea-battle of
Dan-no-ura in 1185. They had no choice but
mass suicide. Led by Antoku's grandmother,
carrying him in her arms, all the leading Taira
warriors jumped overboard in their armour,
and drowned.

Tokugawa Ieyasu (1543–1616 AD)

Samurai warrior who went on to become one of
the most important figures in Japanese history.
He was born into the age of warring states,
when the country was torn apart by violent
conflict between rival lords. He believed the
daimyo should be brought together under a
single ruler, and formed alliances with others

Samurai Hall of Fame

who felt the same way, like Oda Nobunaga and Toyotomi Hideyoshi. After winning victory in the battle of Sekigahara, Ieyasu became shogun in 1603. The Tokugawa dynasty would last for 250 years.

Tomoe Gozen (1157–1247 AD)

Female samurai known for her skill at archery and sword-fighting. She was appointed as a commander in the Genpei War and led thousands of samurai into bloody battles. It's said that she once fought with just 300 samurai against 2,000 rivals on horseback. Tomoe went on to become an iconic figure in Japan, appearing in Noh and Kabuki plays.

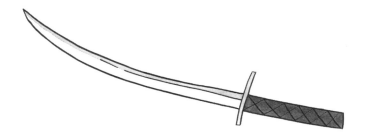

Samurai Hall of Fame

Toyotomi Hideyoshi (*c.1537–1598 AD*)

Samurai warrior who rose up from a low-ranking family to become a powerful politician, though he was never named shogun on account of his humble origins. He made several big changes to Japan, such as forcing samurai to move to castle towns and taking a census and then declaring that everyone had to stay in their areas unless they had permission. This helped to prevent groups of lawless bandits from roaming the country.

Hideyoshi wanted his son to take over when he died. But he was betrayed by fellow samurai Tokugawa Ieyasu, who seized power instead.

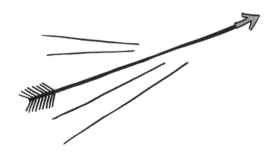

Samurai Hall of Fame

Yamato Takeru (72–? AD)

A brave and cunning prince who had an amazing sword that came from the belly of an eight-headed dragon and which could cut away burning grass. He defeated enemies by dressing up as a woman and killing them when they were drunk. And when he died, he magically transformed into a white bird and disappeared from the world.

As you might have guessed from these 'facts', Takeru was a legendary figure, and the subject of many elaborate folk tales. But his story inspired many genuine samurai.

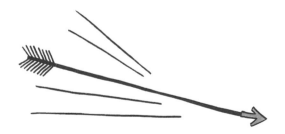

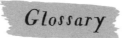

Glossary

Anime
Japanese animated films with bright colours and frantic action sequences. The samurai is a popular figure in anime, and one even features in the oldest surviving Japanese animation made for public showing.

Ashigaru
An ordinary soldier that wasn't of samurai rank, but still fought in a warlord's army.

Bokken
A wooden sword used for training samurai.

Bonsai
The Japanese art of growing small, potted versions of different trees and shrubs.

Glossary

Buddhism
The fourth largest religion in the world, Buddhism grew from the teachings of Siddhārtha Gautama, also known as 'The Buddha'.

Bushido
The name given to the samurai code of honesty, bravery, obedience and loyalty.

Chivalry
The code of honour followed by medieval knights. The European equivalent of Bushido.

Daimyo
Samurai lords who lived in great estates or castles.

Glossary

Edamame
Boiled soya beans served in their pods. The dish was popular in medieval Japan and is still eaten today.

Edo period
The time from 1603 to 1868, when Tokugawa Ieyasu and his descendants ruled from Edo, which is now known as Tokyo.

Judo
A martial art in which opponents use holds and throws to unbalance each other. In English it means 'gentle way'.

Kabuki
A style of popular drama developed in the 17th century which featured elaborate costumes and make-up. It was a blend of music, dance, mime and highly-skilled visual performance.

Karate
A martial art which involves striking an opponent with the hands, knees and feet. In English it means 'empty hand'.

Glossary

Katana
A sword with a long, curved blade with a single edge that was popular with samurai.

Kendo
A martial art in which opponents fence with long sticks. It developed from samurai training methods, and means 'sword way'.

Manga
Comic books of Japanese origin. Samurai feature in many classic manga stories such as *Lone Wolf and Cub*.

Musket
A type of long, heavy gun that was loaded from the front. It was introduced to Japan in the 16th century, but took a while to become established as a samurai weapon.

Glossary

Naginata
Weapon that has a long wooden shaft and a sharp metal blade. These are the weapons most commonly associated with female samurai.

Noh
A traditional form of Japanese drama that featured masks, heavy costumes and stylised movement.

Samurai
Fierce warriors who fought gruesome battles in medieval Japan.

Shinto
Ancient Japanese religion in which people worship ancestors and different nature spirits.

Shogun
The military leader of Japan. He was second in rank to the emperor, and ruled on his behalf.

Zen
A branch of Buddhism popular in Japan. Its followers seek understanding through meditation and self-discipline.

THE LONG-LOST SECRET DIARY OF THE WORLD'S WORST

The Long-Lost Secret Diary of the World's Worst Astronaut
Chosen for the 2019 Summer Reading Challenge.

The Long-Lost Secret Diary of the World's Worst Pirate
Shortlisted for the Lancashire School Library Service Fantastic Book Awards (FBA) 2017–18.

'Although easy to read, the vocabulary is great and the plot lines engaging – excellent reads for developing readers.'
Library Girl and Book Boy Blog

PB ISBN: 978-1-912233-19-9

Tim Collins/ Sarah Horne

PB ISBN: 978-1-912233-20-5

Tim Collins / Isobel Lundie

PB ISBN: 978-1-912537-26-6

PB ISBN: 978-1-912006-67-0

Tim Collins/ Sarah Horne

PB ISBN: 978-1-912006-66-3

Tim Collins / Isobel Lundie

PB ISBN: 978-1-912537-44-0

PB ISBN: 978-1-912904-23-5

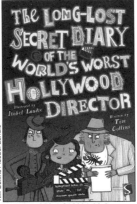

Tim Collins / Isobel Lundie

PB ISBN: 978-1-912904-66-2

Tim Collins / Isobel Lundie

PB ISBN: 978-1-912904-94-5

A selected list of Scribo titles

The prices shown below are correct at the time of going to press. However, The Salariya Book Company reserves the right to show new retail prices on covers, which may differ from those previously advertised.

Gladiator School by Dan Scott

1	Blood Oath	978-1-908177-48-3	£6.99
2	Blood & Fire	978-1-908973-60-3	£6.99
3	Blood & Sand	978-1-909645-16-5	£6.99
4	Blood Vengeance	978-1-909645-62-2	£6.99
5	Blood & Thunder	978-1-910184-20-2	£6.99
6	Blood Justice	978-1-910184-43-1	£6.99

Iron Sky by Alex Woolf

2	Call of the Phoenix	978-1-910184-87-5	£6.99

Shivers by John Townsend

1	Ghost Stories	978-1-912233-52-6	£6.99
2	Pirate Stories	978-1-2233-51-9	£6.99

The Curse of the Speckled Monster
by John Townsend

1	Graverobbers and Gallows	978-1-912233-32-8	£6.99
2	The Twist of the Hangman	978-1-912233-33-5	£6.99

Ballet School by Fiona Macdonald
1. Peter & The Wolf   978-1-911242-37-6   £6.99
2. Samira's Garden   978-1-912006-62-5   £6.99

Aldo Moon by Alex Woolf
1 Aldo Moon and the Ghost
    at Gravewood Hall   978-1-908177-84-1   £6.99

The Shakespeare Plot by Alex Woolf
1 Assassin's Code   978-1-911242-38-3   £9.99
2 The Dark Forest   978-1-912006-95-3   £9.99
3 The Powder Treason   978-1-912006-33-5   £9.99

Visit our website at:

www.salariya.com

All Scribo and Salariya Book Company titles can be
ordered from your local bookshop, or by post from:

The Salariya Book Co. Ltd,
25 Marlborough Place
Brighton
BN1 1UB